C904168086

KU-239-564

For Goldy

BLOOMSBURY CHILDREN'S BOOKS
Bloomsbury Publishing Plc
50 Bedford Square, London, WC1B 3DP, UK
29 Earlsfort Terrace, Dublin 2, Ireland

BLOOMSBURY, BLOOMSBURY CHILDREN'S BOOKS and the Diana logo are trademarks of Bloomsbury Publishing Plc

First published in Great Britain in 2022 by Bloomsbury Publishing Plc

Text and illustrations copyright © Tom Percival 2022

Tom Percival has asserted his rights under the Copyright, Designs and Patents Act, 1988, to be identified as the Author/Illustrator of this work

All rights reserved. No part of this publication may be reproduced or transmitted in any form or by any means, electronic or mechanical, including photocopying, recording, or any information storage or retrieval system, without prior permission in writing from the publishers

A catalogue record for this book is available from the British Library

ISBN 978 1 5266 1302 8 (HB)
ISBN 978 1 5266 1301 1 (PB)
ISBN 978 1 5266 1303 5 (eBook)

1 3 5 7 9 10 8 6 4 2

Printed and bound in China by Leo Paper Products, Heshan, Guangdong

MIX
Paper from
responsible sources
FSC® C020056

To find out more about our authors and books visit www.bloomsbury.com and sign up for our newsletters

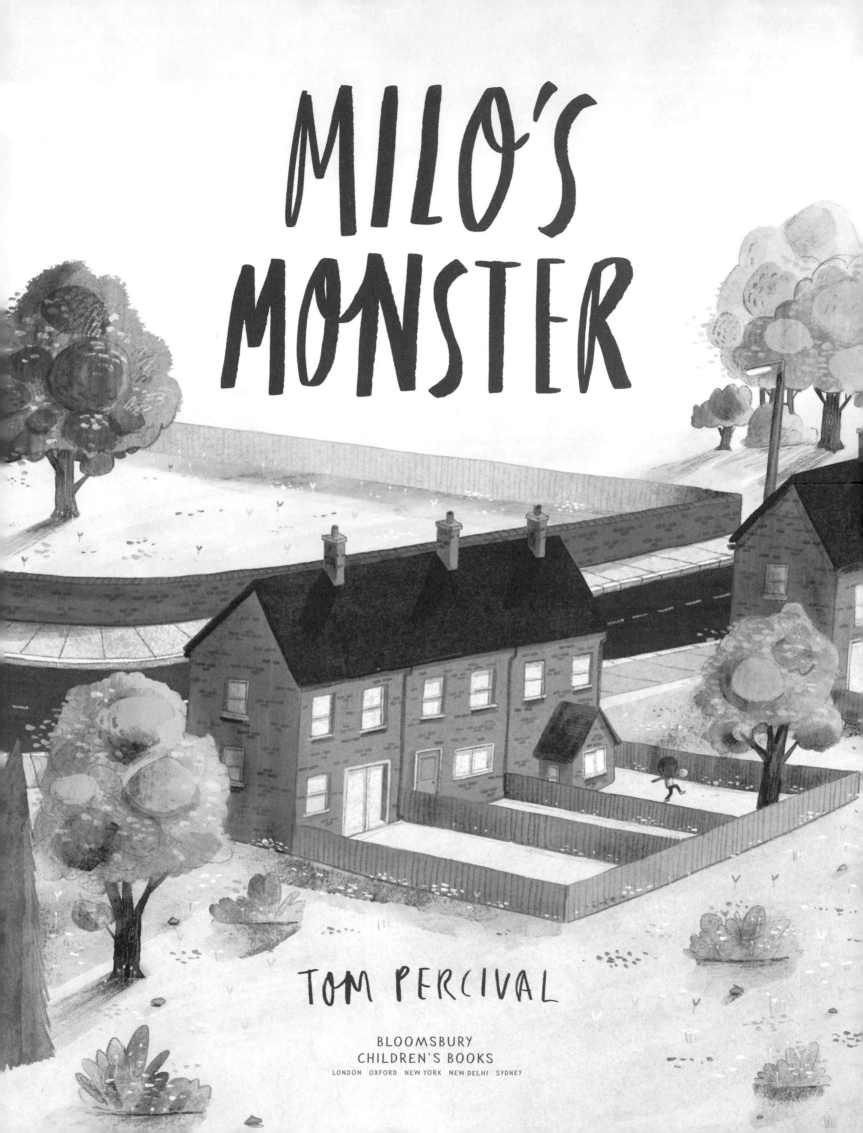

MILO'S MONSTER

TOM PERCIVAL

BLOOMSBURY
CHILDREN'S BOOKS
LONDON   OXFORD   NEW YORK   NEW DELHI   SYDNEY

Nothing could beat the feeling
of having a **best friend**.

Then one day, a new family moved into
the big old house across the road.

Milo watched as a girl ran excitedly around the garden. She smiled and waved, and Milo waved back.

Later that afternoon, Milo went to call for Jay,
but he wasn't in. He had gone over to the
big old house across the road . . .

Without telling Milo.

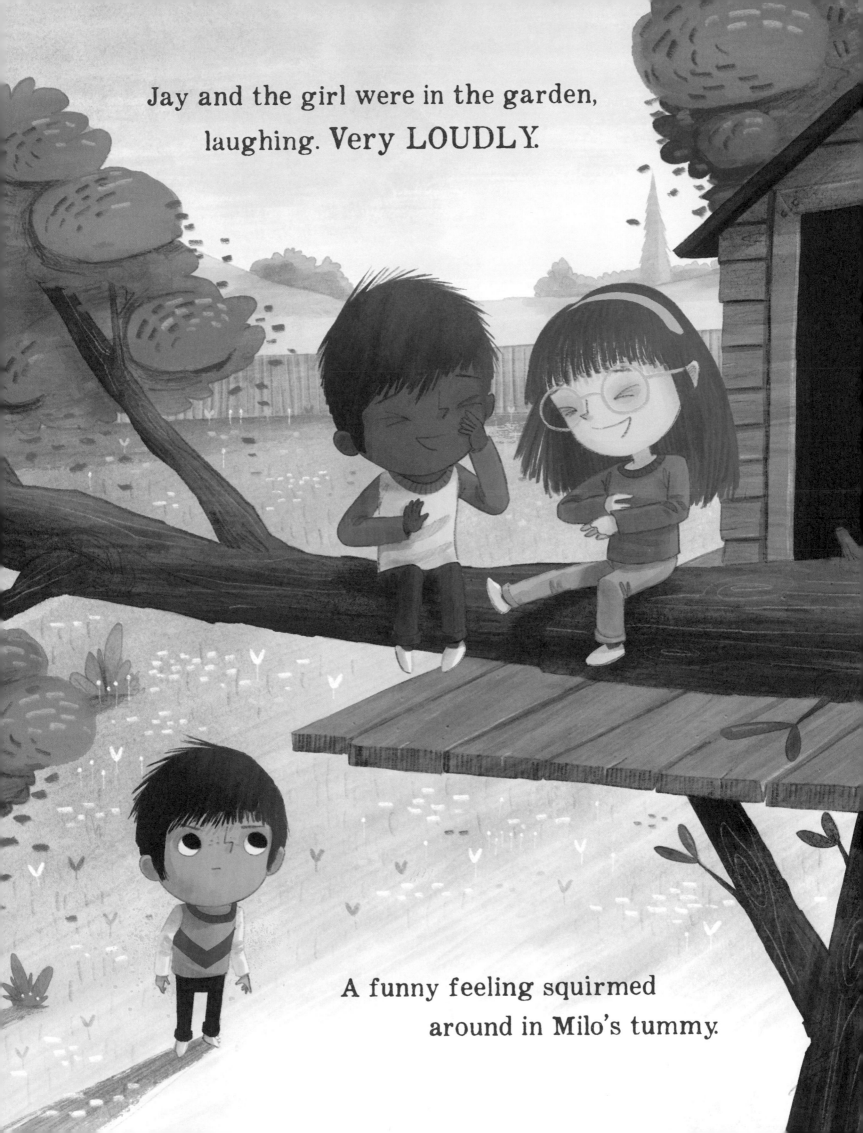

Jay and the girl were in the garden,
laughing. Very LOUDLY.

A funny feeling squirmed
around in Milo's tummy.

"Hi Milo," called Jay. "This is Suzi.
Isn't her garden AMAZING?"

Milo nodded, but the jealous, squirmy feeling was nothing to do with Suzi's massive garden and everything to do with how much fun Jay was having . . .

without him!

The next day, Jay was out, AGAIN.

Milo knew exactly where
he would be . . .

And sure enough, he was outside
reading comics with Suzi.

Then Milo had a horrible thought . . .

What if Jay didn't want to be best friends
with him anymore?

The squirmy feeling took over completely.
And as it did, something very strange happened . . .

A GREEN-EYED
MONSTER
popped up, right beside him.

"IT'S NOT FAIR!" muttered the monster.
"Jay is YOUR friend, not Suzi's!"

From then on, the green-eyed monster
wouldn't leave him alone!

Whenever he saw Jay and Suzi laughing, the green-eyed monster said they were making fun of him.

And whenever he saw them playing . . .

the monster hissed that they were having more fun without him.

Every time Milo saw Suzi and Jay together,
the green-eyed monster made him feel
TERRIBLE.

So, Milo decided to stop seeing them at all.

If they called round at his
house, he pretended
not to be in.

If he saw them at the park,
he would hide.

And if either of them asked what was wrong,
he just said, "Nothing," and turned away.

Day after day, he walked around with only the miserable mutterings of the green-eyed monster for company.

Until one day...

Suzi tapped him on the shoulder.
"Why aren't you and Jay friends anymore?"
she asked. "He really misses you!"

She looked *very* upset.

The monster said it was a trick.
That Suzi was lying.

But Milo shook his head.

It was time to get rid of that pesky monster
once and for all!

Milo shut his eyes tight. He took a deep breath and tried to force the bad feeling away.

The green-eyed monster protested
and muttered mean words –
but its voice became quieter

and quieter,

and quieter,

until at last it was
completely
GONE.

Finally Milo could see the truth.
The green-eyed monster had nearly ruined
EVERYTHING!

Now, he did the only thing that he could.

He said, "I'm sorry."
And he really was.

Soon they were all friends again,
laughing and playing in Suzi's garden –
TOGETHER.

Milo smiled.
Nothing could beat the feeling
of having a best friend . . .

Except having TWO of them!

1

Human–animal interaction – the place of the companion animal in society

Andi Godfrey

Key Points

- The domestication of dogs and cats was a natural progression from man's need for help with guarding, hunting and the herding of livestock and the animal's need for shelter and protection from predators
- The possession of a companion animal can have a beneficial effect on health, child development and helping elderly people to cope with retirement and loss of a spouse
- Companion animals are widely used to provide therapy in prisons, schools, hospitals and hospices
- Nowadays dogs play an essential role in sport and in the service of man

- Civilized society is based on the fundamental principle that where animals are used to accommodate human needs, their welfare is of paramount importance
- Responsible pet ownership is designed to produce an animal that is healthy and well trained and causes no problems to the society and the environment in which it lives
- Pet abuse is an increasingly common problem and may lead to abuse of family members
- Euthanasia is a difficult decision and an emotionally testing time for the client. It is at this time that the veterinary nurse plays a vital role in supporting both the veterinary surgeon and the client

Introduction

Interaction between domestic animals and humans has existed throughout history but it is only within the past 30 years that we have begun to understand the importance of the human–animal bond and how it can influence our society. Research in this field is still in its infancy but many benefits of pet ownership have been proved scientifically. While human–animal interaction does not yet rate highly on the student veterinary nurse's syllabus, it is a subject that is invaluable to those working in practice and in other areas of veterinary medicine. This knowledge will enable veterinary nurses to understand the specific needs of each patient as well as the owner and, consequently, will help to improve the relationship between the practice and the client.

Domestication – how did the wild animal become a pet?

Some people believe the nurturing instinct of the early hunter-gatherers caused them to take the orphans of their prey back to the women to be nursed and, as a result, some animals became tame. Others consider that it was a natural progression from animals being domesticated for utilitarian purposes. Whichever way it came about, it is certain that man and beast formed a symbiotic relationship. Man had the advantage of using animals for transport, security, hunting and keeping down rodent populations, while animals had an easy meal ticket within a community that could also provide them with shelter and protection against predators. As time progressed, animals became more adapted to man's purpose through genetic selection.

Pets have only been referred to as 'companion animals' within the past three decades and it would be reasonable to assume that this new terminology reflects the changing role of domestic animals in modern society. Over 50% of households within the UK now own pets and the vast majority of these animals are kept as companions (Robinson 1995); however, the true reason for introducing the expression 'companion animal' is the belief that the term 'pet' is demeaning (Tannenbaum 1995). The concern for political correctness demonstrates our changing attitude towards animals by suggesting that pets have sensitivities similar to our own. This belief is a far cry from the view of the philosopher Descartes (1596–1650), who decreed that animals had no capacity for reason and therefore could not feel (Dolan 1999).

The concept of keeping animals as companions is not new. There is proof in surviving epitaphs that the ancient Greeks and Romans were avid pet owners and that they revered their pets for their ability to reciprocate affection and provide amusement and companionship. Unlike many other societies, pet owners were from every type of social background rather than being confined to the elite (Bodson 2000). Ancient Egyptian murals depict the enthusiasm that Pharaohs and other high-ranking officials had for keeping dogs, cats and other wild creatures as objects of affection (CSS 1988). In fact, it was thought that the domestic cat originated in Egypt, but archaeologists have since discovered the bones of a cat in Cyprus that are over 9000 years old and all the evidence points to it having been a pet (Muir 2004).

Chinese emperors were reported to have kept pet dogs as early as the 12th century and by the 18th century it was not unknown for puppies to be suckled by human 'wet nurses' and, as adult dogs, to be attended by their own retinue of palace eunuchs (Robinson 1995). This attitude towards dogs was not upheld by the rest of the Chinese population, who were more likely to use dogs for guarding, hunting and as a food source.

In the Western world, during the Middle Ages, animals were considered to be totally utilitarian and any sentiment shown towards them was frowned upon. During the 16th and 17th century, companion animals were cited as evidence of witchcraft. The animals that were thought to be kept as 'familiars' during this period were frequently owned by elderly women who were socially deprived, thus suggesting that in reality these pets were kept for companionship (Robinson 1995). The indications are that dogs gradually worked their way into the affections of humans as a result of their working relationship as hunting dogs, but it is unlikely that they were bred as pets until relatively modern times. During the 18th century, the custom of keeping animals as companions was recognised in the Western world, but this practice was confined to wealthy citizens who could afford to keep non-working animals and were prepared to ignore the common view that showing affection towards animals was both unnatural and immoral. Pet-keeping became fashionable in the Victorian period as a means of getting in touch with the natural world; however, there was little regard for animal welfare at this time and the development of new breeds, for example, is a visible demonstration of man's dominion over nature (Webster 1994, Robinson 1995). Some dogs such as pugs and King Charles spaniels were bred to elicit the 'cute response' and have a paedomorphic appearance to appeal to people's innate parental instinct (Serpell 2003); others were bred simply to achieve a look that was fashionable. In both cases, intensive breeding has resulted in a loss of fitness in the species and in 1994 Bonner reported that genetic disease in pedigree dogs was affecting approximately 142 breeds out of the 170 that were registered with the UK Kennel Club.

Historically, cats appear to have suffered less at the hands of man. Their only function in society was to control the rodent population; thus, no genetic modification was required. Differences in cat species tend to relate to the country from which they come. For example, British short-hair cats are stockier and have thicker coats, whereas those from warmer countries, such as the Siamese, tend to be more slender with long legs and thin tails. This complies with the Darwinian theory of natural selection that species become adapted to their environment. It was not until the 19th century that cats were differentiated into breeds and, following the first cat show held at the Crystal Palace in 1871, standards of excellence were introduced (Thorne 1992).

The advances that have been made in veterinary medicine, the increase in the number of pet insurers, the growth in the pet food industry and the demand for animal behaviourists, personal trainers and alternative therapists suggest how greatly humans value their pets in the present day (Blacker 2004). Domestic animals still have a variety of roles (Table 1.1) but the modern world dictates a greater need for animals to be kept solely as companions. The contributory factors to this requirement are the breakdown of the family unit, a more stressful lifestyle and the fact that more people live alone. For many years pet owners have eulogized the virtues of their animals but it is only recently that scientists have been able to prove that companion animals are beneficial to human health and wellbeing.

Table 1.1 **Reasons for pet-keeping, related to species**

Reason	Species
Decoration	Exotic birds, tropical fish, goldfish, koi carp
Breeding and showing	Dogs, cats, horses, budgerigars – most pet species may be involved
Hobby	All pet species
Child's 'toy'	Ponies, small rodents, rabbits, guinea pigs, goldfish, terrapins
Adult's 'toy'	Horses, dogs, cats, rats, rabbits
Sport	Dogs, horses, pigeons
Status symbols	Rare and expensive breeds of cat and dog, exotic reptiles, tarantulas
Companionship	Dogs, cats, horses, parrots, budgerigars, rabbits and other small rodents
Helpers	Working and service dogs
Money-makers (illegally or legally)	Dogs, cats and exotic species